Written by
**Mindy Atwood**

Illustrated by
**Paul Schultz**

# The Boy in the Golden Cape

FriesenPress

One Printers Way
Altona, MB R0G 0B0
Canada

www.friesenpress.com

Illustrations by Paul Schultz

ISBN
978-1-03-915927-3 (Hardcover)
978-1-03-915926-6 (Paperback)
978-1-03-915928-0 (eBook)

*1. JUVENILE FICTION, SOCIAL ISSUES, FRIENDSHIP*

Distributed to the trade by The Ingram Book Company

This book is dedicated first and foremost to my son, Jason.
It is his bravery and strength as a childhood cancer warrior that
inspired me to write this book.

I also dedicate this book to all childhood cancer warriors,
past and present, who show the world what the meaning of
courage truly is. They, are the superheroes of the world.

"There is a superhero inside all of us.
We just need the courage to put on the cape."
~ Superman

Billy and Jason
were the best of friends...

Actually, they **are** the best of friends!
This is where their story starts, not where it ends.

**B**illy and Jason lived next door to each other, and were best friends. When they first met Jason only came to visit on holidays, but after a while he began living with his dad and Gran next door. Billy loved it when they moved in because he got to spend more time with his best friend. His mom always laughed when he told people Jason was his forever best friend, because they were only seven years old. It's not hard to have a forever best friend when you are only seven.

Jason's room was on the second floor, and had a big window that faced Billy's room. Jason's dad helped them run a trolley between the windows so that they could pass notes, snacks, and secret information back and forth. It was like having their own clubhouse.

Billy's dad gave them each a tablet with a camera. The boys could use the tablets to talk to each other when they weren't together. The tablets didn't get a lot of use, of course, because they were together more than apart. They pretty much only brought them out when one of them was sick or out of town.

The truth was, Billy and Jason did **everything** together. They were in the same class at school, went to vacation bible school every summer, and took swimming and karate lessons together. They played on the same tee-ball teams, and were even in the same Boy Scout troop. They were **always** together—they were inseparable.

This school year, Billy and Jason were in third grade. Their teacher, Mrs. Golay, let them sit next to each other as long as they promised to do their school work, not talk about their plans for recess.

Finding each other was the **greatest** thing that had ever happen to Billy and Jason. They promised each other they would always be friends, and would never be apart...but sometimes, promises are hard to keep.

Jason and his dad went back to their old city for the Thanksgiving break. Jason couldn't **wait** to see his friend and tell him about everything that had happened when he was gone. But that Monday, when Billy went to sit at his desk...there was no sign of Jason.

"Where's Jason?" Billy asked Mrs. Golay.

"He's going to be out for a while," she told Billy. "I'll tell the class more about it soon."

Billy left school that afternoon at a run. But instead of going to his house, he ran to Jason's. Gran opened the door. Her smile looked sad. "Oh, Billy, honey," she said. "I'm sorry. Jason isn't feeling well. He can't have visitors right now."

Billy just stood there, staring at Gran. He didn't know what to think.

"Maybe you should talk to your mom, Billy. She'll explain what's going on."

Billy turned around to leave, but he looked back over his shoulder as he went. "Please tell Jason he's my **forever best friend**...even if he is sick."

Billy ran as fast as he could for home. He jumped the front steps two at a time and raced through the front door. Slightly out of breath, Billy yelled,

# "Mom!"

"In here, Billy," her quiet voice answered from the kitchen.

Billy ran into the kitchen. He was surprised to see both his mother and his father sitting at the kitchen table.

## "What's wrong with Jason?"

The words flew out of his mouth.

His mother motioned him to sit down. She slid a glass of milk and some cookies in front of him. "Jason is sick, honey."

**"I know that!"** Billy felt a whole lot of emotion at once: anger, confusion, but most of all, sadness.

**"What's wrong with him? Can't he be my best friend anymore?"**

"Oh, of course he can, Billy!" his mother said. "Just not right now."

Reaching over, his mother took his hand. She had tears on her cheeks, and it scared him. "Billy..." She took a deep breath. "Jason has a Wilms Tumor. It's a kind of childhood cancer."

**"Cancer?"** Billy had heard of cancer before, but he wasn't sure where. "Is that bad?"

"It can be." His mother wiped the tear from her cheek. "But the children's hospital here is very good, and Jason will get the very best treatment and care."

**"Will he still go to school?"** Billy felt like he was going to cry, but he didn't want to. He looked over at his dad, but he was just staring down at the table, not saying a word. "Dad?"

His dad shook his head, but kept looking down.

"We're not sure yet, honey," his mom said. "But I promise we'll let you know as soon as we know more."

Billy ran up to his room. He turned on his tablet and checked the camera. Jason wasn't online. Billy went to the window, but Jason's shade had been drawn down.

Going to his stash of clubhouse pens, he grabbed one and wrote a quick note to Jason.

"Jason, you are my forever best friend.

I will always be your friend,
and I know you will always be mine.

Please get well soon...

I miss you."

Billy put the note in the trolley and sent it slowly over to Jason's window. He knew that if he could, Jason would get the note.

Laying on his bed, Billy tried to go over all of the words he had heard that day about Jason. **Cancer, sick, hospital, promise . . .** he had heard that last word, promise, a lot. Billy hoped that everyone's promises did come true.

For Jason's sake.

The next few days went by very slowly for Billy. He watched for Jason in the window, but he never saw him. He did see a boy visiting, even though his mom told him Jason wasn't allowed visitors. The boy was bald, and Jason had curly blond hair, so it couldn't have been him. That made Billy angry. Why would Jason have someone else over, and not him? He tried to talk to his dad about it, but his dad got quiet every time Billy said Jason's name.

He tried calling Jason on the house phone a few times, but Gran always said he wasn't able to talk. She promised that she would let Jason know that Billy was calling. But that wasn't the same as talking to his best friend.

A few weeks after Jason left school, Mrs. Sebastian, the school nurse, came in to talk to them. She told them she was there to answer any questions the class had about Jason. Boy, were there a lot of questions!

"Mrs. Sabastian?" Joey was always the first to ask questions no matter what the subject. **"What *is* cancer?"** He seemed proud of his question.

"Well, Joey, cancer is a disease caused by abnormal cell growth." She looked at their teacher, then continued. "Do you remember learning in science a bit about cells and their growth?"

18

"Cancer is when your cells don't work properly. That makes people very sick. Jason's cancer started in his kidney."

A hand in the back was waving wildly. It was Hailey.

### "Mrs. Sebastian? Is cancer contagious? Is there medicine for it? Will Jason always have cancer? Is . . ."

She stopped to take a breath and Mrs. Sabastian jumped in quickly to answer.

"Wow, good questions, Hailey." The nurse pulled up a seat and spoke softly to the class. "No, cancer is not contagious. Yes, there is medicine for it, and Jason is on very strong medicine. That's one of the reasons he can't to come to school or play with his friends."

Mrs. Sebastian stood up, and as she did Hailey yelled,

## "Will he always have it?"

"That's a question I don't have the answer to, Hailey. We hope not, but we'll have to wait and see."

She picked up a pile of papers and asked Mrs. Golay to pass them out. "I have a paper for your parents to read. If you have any more questions after today, you can ask your parents. You're also welcome to stop in and talk to me any time. I know this is scary for everyone—so let's be there for each other, okay?"

On his way home from school that day, Billy thought of a whole lot of questions for his mom. His mother had kept her promise, and she had been telling him everything she knew, but now he had new questions for her.

They sat down together on Billy's bed, and she answered all of the questions that she could. She even explained things he hadn't thought.

"Jason isn't having another friend over but not you, honey. The bald kid you saw in the window **was** Jason. The medicine he's on makes his hair fall out. It will grow back when he's done taking the medicine."

Billy had one more question; it was a question he was afraid to ask.

"Why doesn't Jason want to talk to me?" Billy asked quietly.

"Oh, honey." His mom gave him a big hug. "Jason been in the hospital, and he's really tired. He's not feeling up to talking right now. But I'm sure that he misses you as much as you miss him. And I hope he will be able to talk to you again, soon."

Billy wiped away a few tears. "Why doesn't Dad want to talk to me about Jason?"

His mom thought for a minute then said, "Sometimes people don't know what to say, so they don't say anything. That doesn't mean they don't care."

Sadly, his mother's answers didn't make things easier.
Billy still missed his best friend **terribly**.

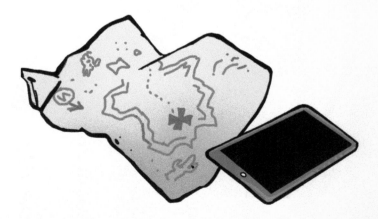

As time passed, lots of people did nice things for Jason and his family. They brought them food, had car washes to help with their medical bills, and the sixth-grade boys even shaved their head to raise money and awareness.

There were childhood cancer awareness gold ribbons hung up throughout the town, gold ribbon bows tied on tree branches, and even a poster of Jason wearing a golden cape asking people to support childhood cancer research.

Billy wanted to do something **extra special** for his best friend, but he wasn't sure what to do.

Then, one day, Billy saw Jason through the window. He was still bald, and he looked tired, but he smiled at Billy. Then he waved and pointed to the trolley. He was finally sending a note back!

The trolley floated across the top of the fence smoothly, stopping just outside Billy's window. He opened the window and pulled it into his room. The note Jason had left in the trolley was simple. It said,

"Hello, best friend. I miss you."

Billy ran to the clubhouse pens, grabbed some paper, and wrote back,

## "I miss you, too!"

He put the note in the trolley and sent it back, just like before Jason was sick.

When Jason opened his window to catch the trolley, Billy saw he had on the shiny golden cape. The cape had a sparkle that caught the light, and seemed magical. It made him look like a golden superhero.

From that day on, Billy and Jason went back to talking on the clubhouse tablets, passing notes across the fence, and planning for all the fun they would have once Jason was better.

Billy even started drawing pictures of Jason wearing the golden cape at the bottom of their notes. He gave him the nickname, "the Boy in the Golden Cape." When Billy heard from his mom that Jason might get to come back to school soon, he couldn't have been more excited! He desperately wanted to do something **special** for Jason, but still couldn't think of anything...

## Then an idea hit him.

That afternoon, after school, Billy gathered up all of his courage. He asked three of his neighbors if he could walk their dogs, for a fee. He didn't tell them what he wanted the money for, just that it was special.

He walked the dogs (with his mom or dad) for two weeks straight, until he had enough for his special surprise for Jason. He'd need his mom's help, but she was always good at helping. He was going to pull this off!

Billy sketched out his plan, gathered his supplies, and went to work. The only people who knew about his surprise were his mom, Gran, and Mrs. Golay.

The end of the school year was getting close, and Billy worked hard to make sure the surprise was ready for Jason's return to school. Every day he waited patiently, sort of, to hear when Jason would be coming back to school. He asked Jason each time they talked, but Jason didn't know either.

Finally, Gran said she had a surprise for him—and he just knew it had to be Jason's **return day!**

At 8:45 a.m. the next day, with the sun shining in the sky, close to the end of the school year, Jason came out of the house and down the steps. He couldn't walk to school just yet, but Billy was allowed to ride with him in the car.

**It was like no time had passed!** The boys were so busy making new plans for the summer that they didn't even notice when they arrived at the school.

Jason had to check into the office and talk with the school nurse before going to class, and that gave Billy enough time to run down and get his surprise ready. His heart was beating so hard he could barely talk. Mrs. Golay knew that it was **"go time,"** so she helped get the surprise ready.

A little while later, there was a knock on the classroom door. Jason, his dad, Gran, the principal, the school nurse, and a newspaper reporter walked into the room. The roar of the kids when they saw Jason was so loud that all of the other classes cheered as well. They knew that sound meant that Jason must be back!

Jason stood staring at the class. There was a huge banner above the window. It read, **"Welcome back, Jason** . . . the Boy in the Golden Cape!"** The entire class were wearing their own golden capes, in honor of Jason's time fighting childhood cancer.

Billy handed Jason the original golden cape, which Gran had brought from home. Billy had saved up enough money to do the banner, buy a cape for all of their classmates, and have the words,

## "To my life-long best friend, the Amazing Boy in the Golden Cape,"

embroidered on the back of Jason's cape.

Billy's mom secretly had the words, **"Forever best friend of the Boy in the Golden Cape,"** embroidered on the back of Billy's cape, too.

The rest of the school year, and into the summer, Billy and Jason wore their golden capes **every day.** Every week, their classmates wore theirs to a new club they started called the Golden Cape Club. Their mission was to raise money and awareness for childhood cancer research.

The reporter who had written a story about Jason's childhood cancer journey, and return to school, did another story about their club. The picture on the front page was Jason and Billy in their special golden capes.

Like I said at the beginning of the book, Jason and Billy are still the **best** of friends. And if you ever visit their neighborhood, you just might see two new little guys running along in their

golden capes . . .